This book belongs to

_____

WHO'S AFRAID OF THE BIG BAD MOP?

A Lesson in Handling Fear

by Doug Peterson   Illustrated by Greg Hardin
and John Trent

SCHOLASTIC INC.

New York Toronto London Auckland Sydney
Mexico City New Delhi Hong Kong Buenos Aires

Ladies and gentlemen,
the story you are about to read is silly.
The names have been changed to
protect the serious.

It was a slow day at police headquarters. Bob worked on a puzzle,
while I read a book: *The Mop That Ate Cleveland*. The book was

It was pretty scary stuff. But it didn't bother me. After all, I was a detective.

My name is Detective Larry the Cucumber, and my partner is Bob the Tomato. Bob carries a badge. I carry a badger. Don't ask why.

12:53 p.m. I was just getting to the scariest part of my book when all of a sudden—

RINNNNNG!

"AHHHHHHHHHHHHH!"

The phone call startled me, and I nearly jumped out of my skin.

"I'm not scared," I told Bob, as I started to climb down from the filing cabinet. "I was just seeing how high I can jump."

Detectives never know when they will have to jump.

As it turned out, the phone call was important. Annie had disappeared from Veggie Valley Elementary School. She had vanished without a trace!

1:05 p.m. We arrived at Veggie Valley Elementary School. Although it was Saturday, the school was buzzing with people. It was the day of the big City Spelling Bee.

"Can you tell us what happened?" Bob asked Principal Petunia.

"Just the facts, ma'am," I added. "And by the way, *facts* is spelled *F-A-X*." In my day, I was quite the speller.

Judges

Petunia tried to tell me that the word *facts* was spelled
F-A-C-T-S. Can you believe it?

Then Petunia went on, "Our spelling bee is supposed
to start at two o'clock. Annie is one of the school's best
spellers. But she's gone!"

"*Gone*. That's spelled *G-A-W-N*,"
I said, writing in my notebook. But
Petunia tried to tell me that *gone*
was spelled *G-O-N-E*.
Can you believe it?

"Do you have any idea why Annie disappeared?" Bob asked the girl's parents, as they showed us her picture.

"Well, Annie does have a bad case of stage fright," said Annie's dad.

"Very interesting," I said. "How long has Annie been afraid of stages?"

"She *isn't* afraid of stages," said Annie's mom. "Stage fright means she's afraid of getting up in front of lots of people—like at this spelling bee."

12

Whenever Annie is afraid, she hides," added her dad. "We've tried to teach her that whenever she's afraid, she should talk to God or to us."

"It must be tough being scared," I said. "I'm glad we detectives are never afraid." Bob just rolled his eyes.

1:15 p.m. Bob searched the first floor of the school, while I checked upstairs. I began by looking inside the first-grade classroom, which was empty. No sign of Annie.

Then I went to the second-grade classroom—still no Annie.

Finally, I peeked inside the third-grade classroom. That's strange, I thought to myself. The room was very dark and seemed to be filled with lots of stuff.

"It's a good thing we detectives are never afraid," I reminded myself as I walked into the spooky room.

1:28 p.m. Fumbling around,
I finally found the light switch.

CLICK!

"AHHHH!"

I found myself staring at a huge mop.
Was *this* the Mop That Ate Cleveland?
And was *this* mop about to wipe me off
the face of the Earth?

Then it dawned on me. I wasn't inside the third-grade classroom.
I was inside the janitor's closet with lots and lots of mops!

"AHHHHHHHHHHHHH!"

I turned to run but tripped over a bucket and crashed against a rolled-up hose. The hose curled around me like a snake.

With the hose wrapping me up, I yanked the door handle, and . . . The handle came off! I was trapped in a janitor's closet with the Mop That Ate Cleveland and the Garden Hose of Doom! I bumbled backward against the wall.

Then another stringy mop fell right into my face, knocking me over! When I tried to get up, paper towels spilled on top of me. Now I was being attacked by paper towels!

Then a bucket toppled onto my head! Unable to see, I ran straight into a shelf!

With the bucket still on my head, I dashed toward the door.
I wanted to bust through. I wanted to—

"WHOOOOOOOAAAAA!"

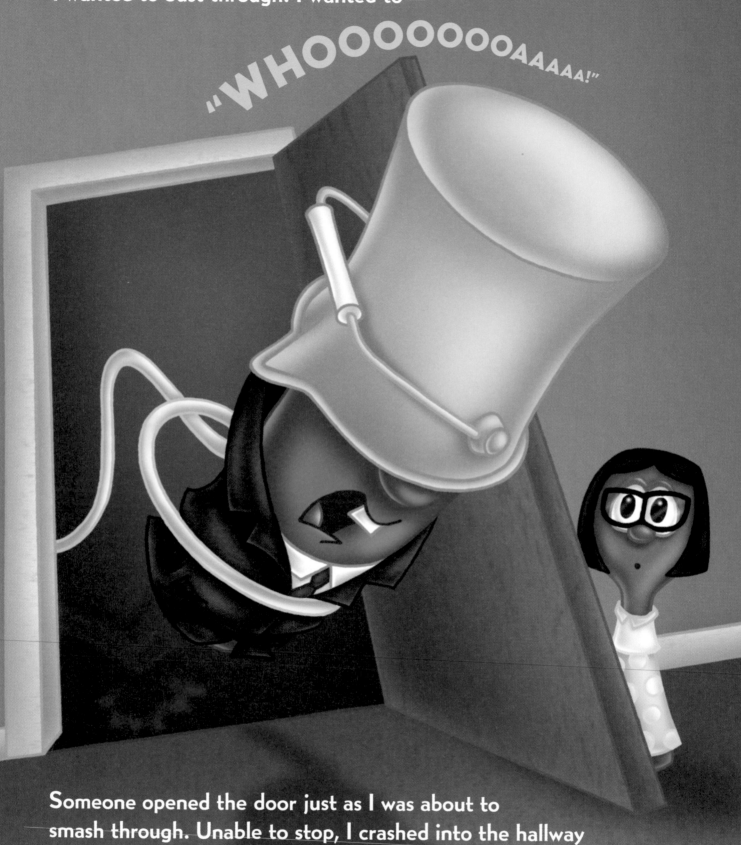

Someone opened the door just as I was about to
smash through. Unable to stop, I crashed into the hallway
wall and wound up in a crazy heap on the floor.

"Are you all right?" asked a girl, as she lifted
the bucket from my head.
  I found myself looking right into Annie's face.

1:45 p.m. Bob, Petunia, and Annie's parents rushed over.

"What's all the racket?" asked Bob.

"We heard the noise and—*Annie*!"

When everyone spotted Annie, they were shocked and overjoyed.

"Where have you been?" asked her mom.
"I've been praying," Annie said.
"But then I heard a noise coming from the janitor's closet, and that's when I found Detective Larry."

From the floor, I gave a weak smile.
"Anyone need their floor waxed?"

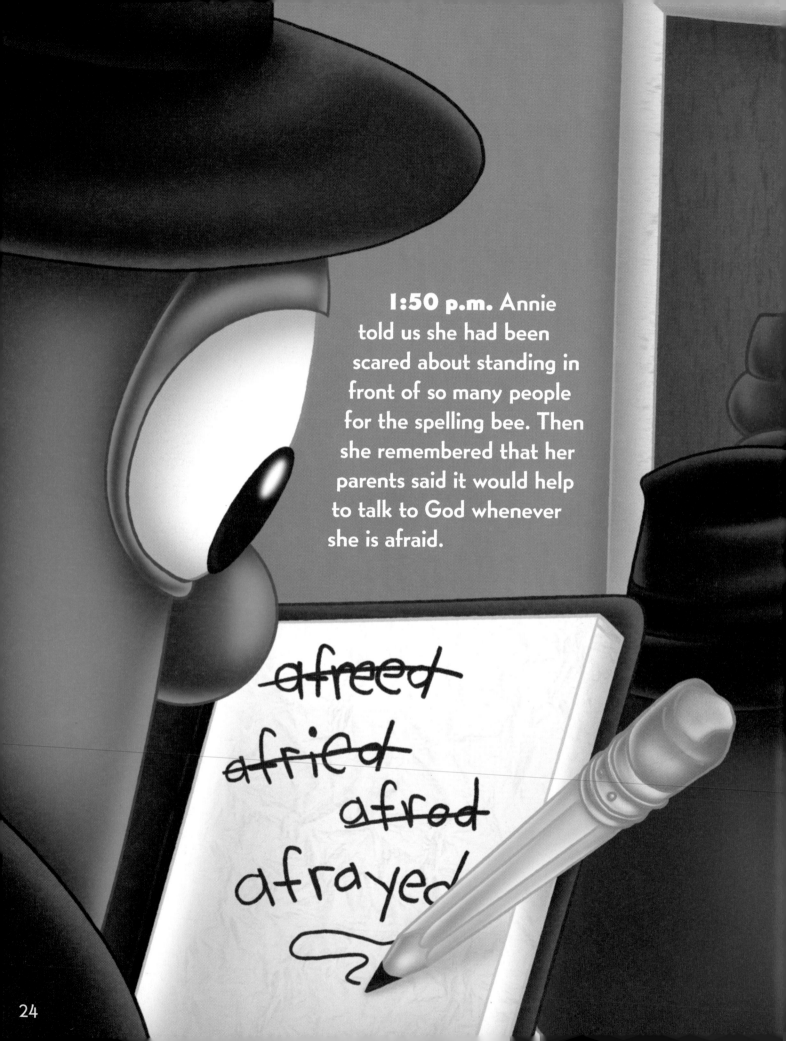

1:50 p.m. Annie told us she had been scared about standing in front of so many people for the spelling bee. Then she remembered that her parents said it would help to talk to God whenever she is afraid.

afreed

affried

afrod

afrayed

"So I went into an empty classroom to pray," said Annie. "And you know what? It helped. It *really* helped to tell God about my fears."

I made a note of that. "Afraid is spelled *A-F-R-A-Y-E-D*," I said. But Petunia tried to tell me that *afraid* is spelled *A-F-R-A-I-D*.
Can you believe it?

3:00 p.m. The spelling bee was over, and Annie did great. She still had some butterflies in her belly, but she stood in front of the crowd anyway. What a brave girl!

Although Annie didn't win the spelling bee, she came away with the third-place ribbon. In fact, the only thing that went wrong during the entire spelling bee was when Junior Asparagus was asked to spell *mop*.

That's when I ran out of the room screaming.
But then I remembered. I could talk to God when I am afraid.
And that really helped!
Can you believe it?